THE LITTLEST BOOK
OF LOVE AND FRIENDSHIP

by Danielle Denega
illustrated by Jim Talbot

SCHOLASTIC INC.

New York   Toronto   London   Auckland   Sydney
Mexico C   CONNETQUOT PUBLIC LIBRARY   Aires
760 OCEAN AVENUE
BOHEMIA, NEW YORK 11716
Tel: (631) 567-5079

For Quigley, my puppy love — D.D.

ISBN-13: 978-0-439-89751-8
ISBN-10: 0-439-89751-3

Littlest Pet Shop © 2007 Hasbro.
LITTLEST PET SHOP and all related characters
and elements are trademarks of and © Hasbro.
All Rights Reserved.

Published by Scholastic Inc. SCHOLASTIC and associated logos
arc trademarks and/or registered trademarks of Scholastic Inc.

12 11 10 9 8 7 6 5 4 3 2 1   7 8 9 10 11/0

Interior book design by Two Red Shoes Design

Printed in Singapore
First printing, January 2007

Friends Rule!

FRIENDS QUIZ!
HOW WELL DO YOU KNOW ME?

Grab a friend, two sheets of paper, and two pens. Without talking about it with your friend, write down answers to the following questions. Then swap papers with your friend and "grade" your quizzes to see how well you know each other!

✳ My friend's *favorite treat* is...

✳ My friend's middle name is...

✳ My friend's least favorite food is...

✳ My friend wants to be a _____ when she *grows up*.

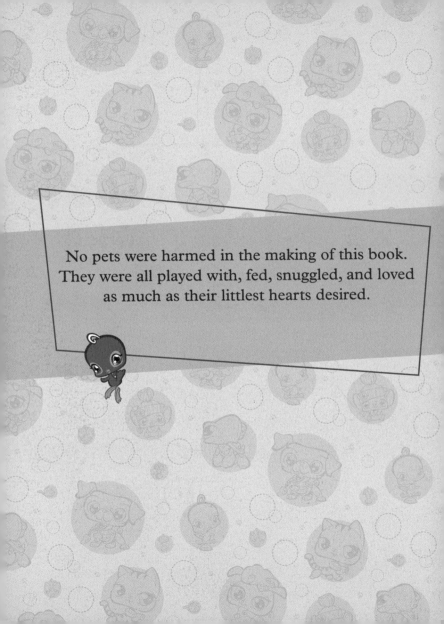

❋ My friend has a **CRUSH** on this person . . .

❋ My friend's favorite *hobby* is . . .

❋ My friend has this many **SIBLINGS** . . .

❋ My friend's **FAVORITE SCHOOL SUBJECT** is . . .

❋ My friend's *eyes* are this color . . .

❋ My friend's *favorite pet* is . . .

MONKEYING AROUND:
Fun Things TO DO WITH FRIENDS

❋ Go for a bike ride.

❋ Start a **book club**. Read the same book and talk about it together.

❋ Make **crafts** together. Try the friendship bracelets on page 6!

❋ Have a *slumber party*.

❋ Put on a *play* that you write yourselves.

❋ Keep a **notebook** or **online journal** about your friendship.

Hold tight

to a true friend
with both paws.

MAKE A
Friendship
BRACELET

**Show your friends you love them by
making them friendship bracelets.**

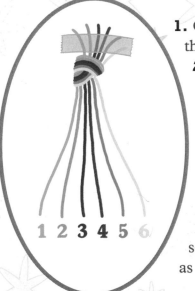

1 2 **3 4** 5 6

1. Cut embroidery
thread into *six
24-inch (60 cm)
strands.* Gather the
six ends together
and tie a knot at
the top. Arrange
them in the order
you would like for
your bracelet. Tie
the knotted end to
something firm, such
as a bedpost or chair.

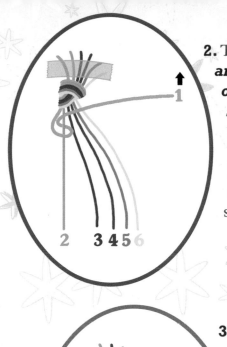

2. Take ***strand 1 and wrap it over and around strand 2*** to make a knot. Tighten by holding strand 2 and pulling up on strand 1.

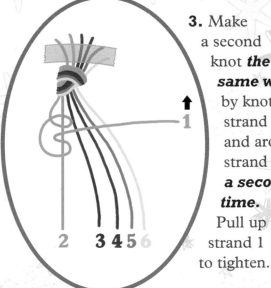

3. Make a second knot ***the same way*** by knotting strand 1 over and around strand 2 ***a second time.*** Pull up on strand 1 to tighten.

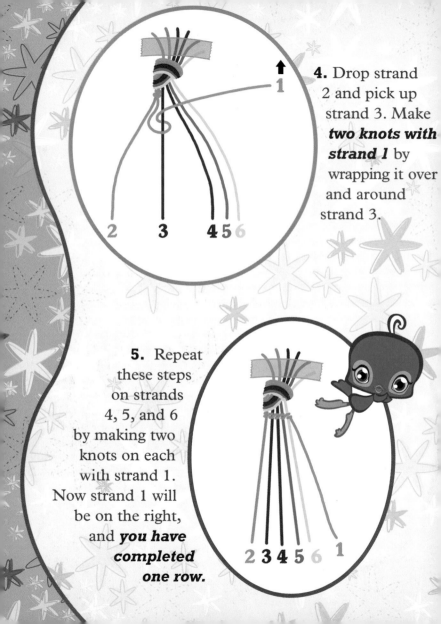

4. Drop strand 2 and pick up strand 3. Make **two knots with strand 1** by wrapping it over and around strand 3.

5. Repeat these steps on strands 4, 5, and 6 by making two knots on each with strand 1. Now strand 1 will be on the right, and **you have completed one row.**

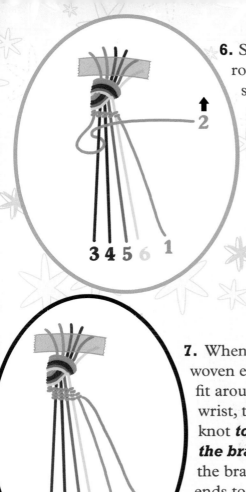

6. Start the next row by taking strand 2 and *making two knots* over and around strands 3, 4, 5, 6, and 1.

7. When you have woven enough to fit around your wrist, tie another knot *to complete the bracelet.* To wear the bracelet, tie the two ends together and trim off the extra strings.

9

TOP FIVE REASONS WHY FRIENDS ARE THE Cat's Meow

1. Friends know your faults and like you anyway.

2. Your friends can help get you through hard times.

3. Every experience is more fun with a friend.

4. Kitty comrades care about you. That makes any day better!

5. They can always be counted on (to scratch behind your ears)!

Good friends

will always share!

TEN TIPS FOR BEING A GOOD FRIEND

1. **Tell her about it!** As often as you can, remind your friend that you're grateful for her friendship.

2. **Keep in touch!** Stay in frequent contact with friends.

3. Be a *good listener.*

4. **Respect the fact that you and your friends are DIFFERENT.** Embrace these differences and learn from them!

5. **Forgive and forget.** If you have a disagreement with a friend, say you're sorry. Or accept an apology from your friend. Then move on!

6. Try to *understand* your friends' feelings and moods, and they will do the same for you!

7. Flattery will get you everywhere. Tell a friend she is talented or smart. It's sure to make her feel great, and she'll want to return the compliment!

8. Always treat friends the way *you want to be treated* yourself.

9. Be **TRUSTWORTHY.**

10. Spread good cheer. If your friend is upset, try to make her feel better.

PET PEEVE:

Don't be cliquey or exclusive! Include new people in your activities. Who knows? That person may become a new friend!

Lots of Fish in the Sea:
How to Make New Friends

Be Brave

I'M USUALLY VERY TIMID.
BUT THAT DOESN'T MEAN YOU HAVE TO BE!
WHEN YOU MEET NEW MICE,
BE CONFIDENT.
A SMILE AND A FRIENDLY FACE WILL MAKE
OTHER MICE COME TO YOU!

TAKE A LEAP: Just Say HELLO

If you find yourself in a new place,
try just saying hi to people.
Then introduce yourself and explain that you're new.
You'll be surprised at how far it will go
in making new friends!

17

NEW SCHOOL

You might find yourself in a new school of fish one day. Here are some ideas to help you meet new friends:

* Join a **CLUB OR TEAM** (like the swim team).

* Ask the teacher to introduce you to some of the other fish.

❋ Sit down next to someone friendly-looking at lunchtime.

❋ Offer to help someone. It could be with an assignment, a dance move, or some fashion tips!

PET PEEVE:

Don't Be a Show-off!

Nobody likes the class clown fish, know-it-all, or pet that thinks they're the best at everything—especially when it's the new hamster in the house. Let others have the spotlight once in a while!

THE DOG NEXT DOOR:
Meet the Neighbors

If you move to a new place, try barking and scratching at the neighbor's door. Have an adult walk you over for an introduction. There might be a puppy your age that lives there. Or the adult that lives there may tell you about other puppies that live nearby.

PRETTY KITTY:
THREE WAYS TO MAKE
a Good First Impression

1. Be sure to *groom well* before meeting new people! Clean hair and clothes will make you look your best.

2. *Be polite!* Say "please" and "thank you" when appropriate.

3. Be a good conversationalist: Speak in turn, listen to others carefully, and give thoughtful responses.

GET THE CONVO
IN MOTION

If you want to meet someone, start by saying hello. Then show you're interested by asking one (or more) of these questions:

❋ **What is your favorite movie?** (Or substitute "Littlest Pet Shop pet" or "band" for "movie.") Asking people about their favorites will tell you if you have things in common, and it's sure to get them talking!

❋ **Who is the best teacher at school?**

❋ **Did you understand the homework assignment?**

❋ **Where is the best place to hang out?** Ask for an opinion to get the lowdown on a new place and begin a conversation.

❋ **WHERE did YOU GET YOUR FABULOUS HAIRCUT?** (Or substitute "tank top" or "jeans" for "haircut.") It'll make her feel great and give you a way to start chatting!

> **You can make more friends in two months by becoming interested in other people than you can by trying to get other people interested in you.**

—Dale Carnegie (1888–1955),
American writer and author of the book
How to Win Friends and Influence People

Long-term Turtles:

How to Maintain Old Friendships

HOW DO YOU KEEP AN OLD FRIEND A
Friend for Life?

❋ Remind her often how **GREAT** she is!

❋ Spend *as much time* with old friends as with new ones. Keep the good times rolling!

❋ *NEVER forget a birthday or special occasion.* Make your friends feel as special as they are by letting them know you remember their special days.

❋ **Keep trying NEW THINGS together.**
Creating new memories with
an old friend will keep
the fun alive.

❋ Include your OLD
FRIEND when you
hang with
your new
ones.

MY DOG PACK

One fun activity to do with your pack of friends is to keep a friends journal where you log all the furry facts about yourselves. Write down things such as how you met, what you like about each other, and what you do to keep the friendship strong –
NOW AND FOREVER!

One of the
GREAT THINGS
about old
friends
is that you
can be silly
with them.

OLD FRIENDS QUIZ!

On a separate sheet of paper, you and an old friend should write down answers to the following questions. Then "grade" your quizzes to see how well you know each other!

✻ We MET on this day . . .

✻ We were DOING THIS activity . . .

✻ The first thing we said to each other was . . .

✻ The reasons we liked each other were . . .

32

✳ The reasons we are *still BFF* are . . .

✳ Our favorite *thing to do* together now is . . .

✳ The funniest **THING WE'VE EVER DONE** together is . . .

A MOMENT IN TIME

Want to capture a moment in time in the life of your friendship? *Make a time capsule!* Ask an adult for permission, then find a container that has a cover, such as an old coffee can with a plastic lid. Next place important or sentimental objects inside. These objects could include things like pictures of you with your friends, and items that are popular at that time (to remind you what was in style).

You might also want to include a letter to yourselves in which you write down your thoughts about the present and your dreams for the future.

Finally, `bury the sealed container` in a place that you can go back to in five, ten, or even twenty years. Or hide it in a place where you won't forget it. After all that time, you and your friends can dig up the time capsule and *remember all of the great things* about your friendship!

PET PEEVE:

Don't Take an Old Friend for Granted

Sometimes it's easy to assume that an old friend will **ALWAYS** be a friend. But friends need TLC to keep their tails wagging. Don't make the mistake of taking an old friend for granted!

Long-Distance:
How to K.I.T.
(Keep In Touch)

Whether side by side or miles apart, good friends are always close to the heart.

FLYING THE COOP

One day you may learn that a good friend is moving **FAR AWAY.** You also might find that you make friends at summer camp, then have to *leave them* when the summer is over. You and your birds of a feather can no longer be together. It's sad to separate from friends, but it doesn't mean these friendships have to end! Just K.I.T.!

KEEP A PAL CLOSE TO YOUR HEART

No matter the reason, if you find yourself far away from your friends, it's super important to **KEEP IN TOUCH!** Friendships need to be nurtured, especially when it's not possible to see each other all the time. **Make efforts** to stay in contact with friends who are far away and they will become *friends for life!*

GIVE HER A HOLLER

The good old phone is a great way to reach out and touch someone. Give your friend a ring every now and again. There's nothing like hearing the chirp of a friend's voice!

SNAIL MAIL

Another great way to K.I.T. with friends is to use snail mail. Never written a letter? Here are some pointers:

✳ **Include a Heading:** It should have your mailing address and the date.

❋ **Include a Greeting:** Say hello to your friend! Many people start with "Dear" and then the person's first name.

❋ **Include Your Message:** Feel free to "chat" about just about anything.

❋ **Include a Closing:** Say good-bye to your friend! Many people use things like "Your friend" or "Best wishes."

❋ **Include a Signature:** Sign your name at the bottom of the letter. It's okay to just use your first name. You can even sign the letter with a nickname!

USE THE INTERNET!

The Internet is a fast and easy way to K.I.T. with other kitties. Always ask a parent, teacher, or librarian for permission to use the Internet. And be certain to correspond only with friends you know and trust.

E-MAIL

E-mail is a way to **COMMUNICATE** over the Internet. It's a great way to write to friends. Just type a message, click SEND, and have the message delivered to your friend's in-box within minutes! **TRY USING FUN TOOLS** such as emoticons and abbreviations (see page 46).

IMING

Instant Messaging, or IMing, is another way to communicate over the Internet. It's just about the fastest way to K.I.T.! After you type a message and send it, your friend will receive it within seconds. It's instant, like the name! And you can see which of your pals are available — IM tells you who's around to chat and who's not.

CHITCHAT

Here are some shorthand ways to write to your friends in e-mails or in IMs.

BRB = be right back
CU = see you
FYI = for your information
G2G = got to go
H&K = hugs and kisses
JK = just kidding
LOL = laughing out loud
LTNT = long time, no type
L8R = later
TTFN = ta-ta for now
TTYL = talk to you later

"A friend is a gift you give yourself."

— Robert Louis Stevenson (1850–1894),
Scottish novelist, poet, and travel writer
and author of the novel *Treasure Island*